OLD BLACK WITCH!

OLD
BLACK WITCH!

by **WENDE** and **HARRY DEVLIN**

illustrated by **HARRY DEVLIN**

PARENTS' MAGAZINE PRESS • NEW YORK

To

OUR SEVEN BLUEBERRY PANCAKE EATERS

1966 Edition

Nicky and his mother had made a long trip to New England. They didn't have much money, and they wanted to buy an old house to turn into a tearoom. Nicky's mother had in mind a special kind of house for the tearoom. She thought it should be old and warm and cosy.

They looked and looked for such a house. At last, they found a man who said he had just the right house for a tearoom. He said it was old and warm and cosy. He really thought it was old and broken-down and dreadful. Nicky and his mother were too tired even to think. They bought the house.

When all the papers were signed, they went out to the house. Nicky's mother opened the squeaky, old door with the rusty key.

The sun had gone down, and the house was dark and chilly. Nicky began to build a fire in the big fireplace. The fire did not start very easily, and puffs of smoke soon filled the room.

Suddenly, SQUAWK! THUMP! And
down from the chimney fell a big, black
mess. It was covered with cobwebs and made

terrible sounds. It stumbled out of the fire-place into the room. From its long, pointed hat to its long, pointed shoes, it was covered with ashes. It was a fright. It was furious. And it was an old black witch.

Old Black Witch glared into Nicky's face.

"Who told you to build a fire in my fire-place?" she shouted, stamping around and shaking her broom. "Jumping Jehosaphat! You've scorched my blasted broomstick!"

"This is our fireplace and our house because we bought it," Nicky said politely. "And what are you doing in our chimney?"

Old Black Witch had expected to see the boy scream in fright and climb the closest curtain. Now, she looked hard into Nicky's face. She pointed a long, crooked finger at the tip of Nicky's nose.

"Boy," she croaked, "this is MY chimney, MY fireplace, and MY house." She looked at her watch.

" Giblets!" she screeched, "I have been asleep for one hundred years. Now, you just ske-daddle. This is MY house. Scoot! Boo! Scat! Run!"

Nicky's mother, who could hardly believe what she saw, now spoke to Old Black Witch.

"We bought this house to make a warm, cosy, little tearoom with red checked curtains, bunches of Sweet William on the tables, and homemade biscuits with honey."

"And blueberry pancakes," added Nicky.

"Bats!" screamed Old Black Witch, "Over my dead body! This house must have big cobwebs in the corners, black curtains, some old toads in the fireplace, and three inches of dust on the floor."

Old Black Witch cracked her knuckles, popped her eyes, and made awful noises.

"Nonsense," Nicky's mother answered calmly.

"Then what will become of me?" muttered Old Black Witch. "There aren't many

old, broken-down houses left, you know."

"Well, if you'd really like to stay, you may have a room in the attic," said Nicky's mother.

Old Black Witch grumbled all the way up to the attic. But after some banging around, she settled down in a little room under the rafters.

Oddly enough, this little room pleased Old Black Witch. The cobwebs hung heavy with dust, and a family of squeaky bats nested near the roof. There the wind blew, the shutters bumped, and the old beams made spooky music.

She would have liked some pets, such as a few spotted toads. Yes, she thought, a couple of spotted toads would have suited her nicely.

Downstairs, Nicky and his mother began the hard work of fixing up the old house. The cleaning, scrubbing, painting and polishing went on for weeks. Old Black Witch wasn't much help. She switched around on her scratchy old broom, flitting

from stair posts to corner cupboards, shriek-
ing and cackling and making rude remarks
about the way things were going.

One evening, she sailed out through a
window so sparkling clean that she thought
it was open. The crash was ear-splitting.

It was like a clap of thunder. It was very
noisy.

Old Black Witch was hopping mad. She
zoomed back into the room, kicked over a

bucket of suds and shook glass out of her broom all over the clean floor.

When Nicky scolded her for half an hour, Old Black Witch just pulled her long, pointed hat over her long, pointed nose and pretended that she was asleep.

Finally, in spite of Old Black Witch, the tearoom was ready, just as it had been planned. There were red checked curtains, and there were bunches of Sweet William on the tables. The homemade biscuits were delicious, and the blueberry pancakes were the best for miles around.

From the very beginning, "The Jug and Muffin" tearoom was a success. Although people had heard that the house was haunted by an old black witch, no one believed such nonsense.

Yet, they wondered who it was that
shouted down from an attic window, "Boo!

Scat, and Ratcha Fratch!" at all the ladies who came to see the clever, new tearoom.

They all waved back at Old Black Witch and said, "How quaint!" and "How sweet!"

One day, Nicky's mother went upstairs and knocked on Old Black Witch's door. "Black Witch, dear. There is an awfully big crowd downstairs, and I need help with the pancakes." Nicky's mother looked very tired.

"Could stir a little," said Old Black Witch.

It had been a hundred years since she had last cooked, but she soon found herself in the kitchen with a nice, clean apron and a lot of eggs, flour and blueberries. Then, with a pinch of this and a pinch of that, Old Black Witch's blueberry pancakes were simply wonderful.

Before long, Nicky's mother let her serve
some of the pancakes. When the customers

stared, Old Black Witch asked them, "What's the matter, dearie? Is my slip showing?" Sometimes she cackled, "Don't worry, I made them myself." That's why some people worried, but they had to admit the pancakes were marvelous.

Old Black Witch was beginning to enjoy all the attention. Soon, she began singing in her cracked voice as she put the pancakes on the tables.

Sometimes she sang,
   "Boil cauldron,
   Make a brew,
   What kind of berries
   Make pancakes blue?"

Or,

"Boil and bubble,
Dance a jig,
If you eat all these,
You're a polka-dot pig!"

Or,

"Snakes and snails
And gophers' knees!
If you think they are bad,
Then just taste these!"

Not all the people who heard
about "The Jug and Muffin"
tearoom were nice, quiet ladies.

Stories of the famous tearoom reached the ears of two very greedy thieves, who decided to pay a visit to the old house.

They made very careful plans. They put on their sneakiest sneakers, and with a final shh-h-h-h, they made their way through the dark. The night was blue, with a great lemon moon peeking through the trees.

It was Old Black Witch who heard them. She tip-toed down from the attic. In the light of that great lemon moon, she saw the thieves shaking money from the sugar bowl into a bag.

Her face wrinkled into a smile, and her eyes glowed in the corner where she hid. Old Black Witch knew evil and believed in it to a point. These were her kind of people.

She was about to cackle, "Go to it, boys,"

when she realized they were stealing from HER. After all, her blueberry pancakes had made the money in the sugar bowl.

Sudden fury made her hop up and down. She banged the floor with her broom.

The greedy thieves were startled and frightened until they saw that Old Black Witch was really quite tiny. They picked her up, sputtering and kicking, and stuffed her in the almost empty flour barrel. Then, they went back to their stealing.

However, the two thieves did not see the lid of the barrel rise. They did not hear Old Black Witch whisper three magic words. They did not see her eyes cross twice and a sudden puff of smoke.

But the thieves suddenly disappeared.

Where they had been, two green-and-brown
toads blinked at each other in the moonlight.

In a twinkling, Old Black Witch scooped
them up in her apron and popped them

into a wooden cage. From then on, Old Black Witch had two strange spotted toads in her room.

Things went along very well for everyone after that. Old Black Witch helped quite often in the tearoom. She demanded days off in which to be nasty, but then, most witches would. Nicky's mother no longer looked tired. Nicky grew rosy in the country air.

Old Black Witch often told stories to Nicky about the bad old days.

"But I know you are really a GOOD witch," he would say, looking at her fondly.

Then Old Black Witch would look out the window, crack her knuckles, and wink at the dusty crow that lived in the mulberry tree.

"Bats!" she would say, "Bats! Crickets!
And snakes' knees!"